Mysterious Monsters

SEARCHING FOR THE WENDIGO

JENNIFER RIVKIN

PowerKiDS
press.

New York

Published in 2015 by The Rosen Publishing Group, Inc.
29 East 21st Street, New York, NY 10010

Produced for Rosen by BlueApple*Works* Inc.
Art Director: Tibor Choleva
Designer: Joshua Avramson
Photo Research: Jane Reid
Editor for BlueApple*Works*: Melissa McClellan
US Editor: Joshua Shadowens

Illustrations: cover, p. 6 Peter Johnston; p. 1 Kresimir Kirasic; p. 4 Luke Denby; p. 8 inset top YorkBerlin/Shutterstock; p. 8 Rainer Lesniewski/Shutterstock; p. 9 Kresimir Kirasic/T.Choleva; p. 10 top, 10 right, 12, 14, 22, 25 Karl Bodmer/ Public Domain; p. 10 left Fotokostic/Shutterstock; p. 14 top George Catlin/ Public Domain; p. 15 Carlyn Iverson; p. 16 Frederic Remington/ Public Domain; p. 17 Andreas Meyer/Shutterstock /J.Avramson; p. 18 top, 18–19 bottom Stocksnapper/ Shutterstock; p. 18 Bocman1973/Shutterstock; p. 19 John Singer Sargent/ Public Domain; p. 21 TsuneoMP/Shutterstock /J.Avramson; p. 23 left, 26 top inset, 26 bottom T. Choleva; p. 23 right Victor Habbick/Shutterstock; p. 27 Bob Orsillo/ Shutterstock; p. 28 bottom Jeff Cameron Collingwood/Shutterstock/T.Choleva

Photo Credits: back cover wallace wainhouse/Shutterstock; p. 6 top hektor2/Shutterstock; p. 7, p. 16 top inset Jeff Cameron Collingwood/Shutterstock; p. 8 top, 26 Robert Crum/Dreamstime; p. 11 Sergey Uryadnikov/Shutterstock; p. 12 top Esp2k/Shutterstock/T.Choleva; p. 12–13 bottom Natthawon Chaosakun/Shutterstock; p. 13 Kiselev Andrey Valerevich/ Shutterstock/J.Avramson; p. 16 top andreiuc88/Shutterstock; p. 20 top J. Avramson; p. 20 left Dan Thornberg/Shutterstock; p. 20 right Kletr/Shutterstock; p. 22 top andreiuc88/Shutterstock; p. 24 top Monkey Business Images/Shutterstock; p. 24 Julien_N/Shutterstock; p. 28 Aleksey Stemmer/Shutterstock; p. 29 background Elena Elisseeva/Shutterstock; p. 29 bottom Golden Pixels LLC/Shutterstock; paper background Fedorov Oleksiy/Shutterstock

Publisher's Cataloging Data

Rivkin, Jennifer.
Searching for the Wendigo / by Jennifer Rivkin.
p. cm. — (Mysterious monsters)
Includes index.
ISBN 978-1-4777-7117-4 (library binding) — ISBN 978-1-4777-7118-1 (pbk.) —
ISBN 978-1-4777-7119-8 (6-pack)
1. Windigos—Juvenile literature. 2. Algonquin Indians— Folklore—Juvenile literature.
3. Monsters—Juvenile literature. I. Rivkin, Jennifer. II. Title.
QL89.R58 2015
001.944—d23

Manufactured in the United States of America

CPSIA Compliance Information: Batch #WS14PK8 For Further Information contact: Rosen Publishing, New York, New York at 1-800-237-9932

TABLE OF CONTENTS

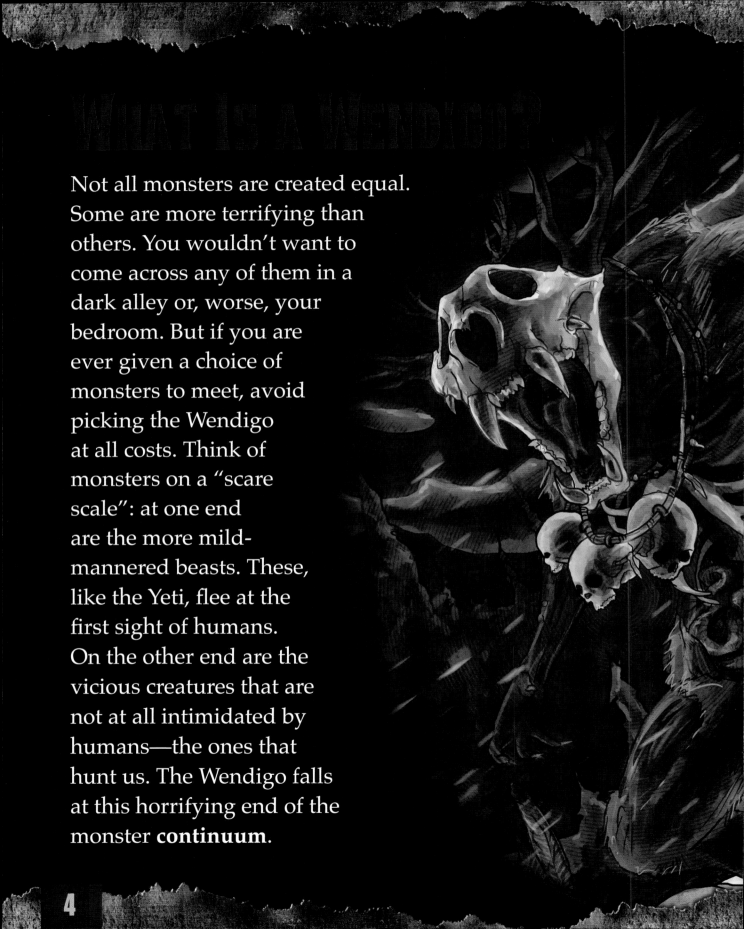

Not all monsters are created equal. Some are more terrifying than others. You wouldn't want to come across any of them in a dark alley or, worse, your bedroom. But if you are ever given a choice of monsters to meet, avoid picking the Wendigo at all costs. Think of monsters on a "scare scale": at one end are the more mild-mannered beasts. These, like the Yeti, flee at the first sight of humans. On the other end are the vicious creatures that are not at all intimidated by humans—the ones that hunt us. The Wendigo falls at this horrifying end of the monster **continuum**.

The name Wendigo (pronounced when-dee-go) comes from the Native American Algonquian languages. There is some debate about the translation of the word. It may mean "evil spirit that devours mankind," "spirit of lonely places," or **"cannibal."** Using any definition, the Wendigo is a creature that is out for human flesh. And it never gets full! No matter how much Wendigo eats, it is always starving . . . and always hunting.

Some people believe the Wendigo is a flesh and blood creature waiting in the woods to capture humans. Others say it is a spirit that possesses humans and turns them into cannibals.

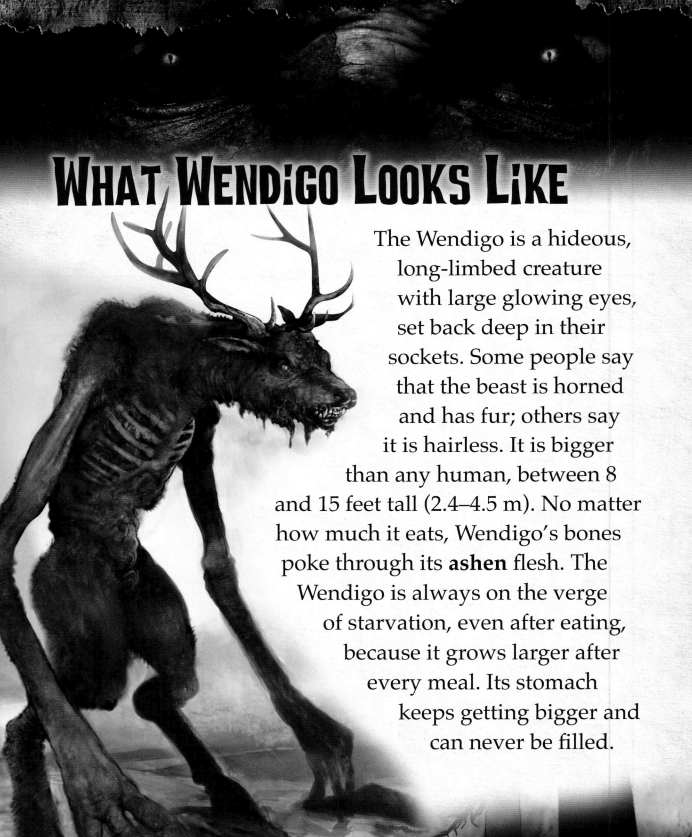

What Wendigo Looks Like

The Wendigo is a hideous, long-limbed creature with large glowing eyes, set back deep in their sockets. Some people say that the beast is horned and has fur; others say it is hairless. It is bigger than any human, between 8 and 15 feet tall (2.4–4.5 m). No matter how much it eats, Wendigo's bones poke through its **ashen** flesh. The Wendigo is always on the verge of starvation, even after eating, because it grows larger after every meal. Its stomach keeps getting bigger and can never be filled.

No Need for Cutlery

It's not hard for the Wendigo to feast. Like many **carnivores**, its body was designed to find, cut, and digest meat. According to legend, the creature has yellowed fangs, razor-sharp claws, and a long tongue. It's nails and teeth can carve through meat like it's butter. One body part is notably absent, however: the Wendigo doesn't have lips . . . because it ate them. The most chilling part of Wendigo's appearance is that it is often covered with the blood of its victims.

Eyewitness Tale

In 1823, Major H. Long, a scout for the US army, visited Lake of the Woods in Ontario, Canada. This was Native American territory. He heard the story about a group of 40 tribe members who were camped on the ridge years before. They began to cannibalize each other when starvation set in. In the end, there was only one woman left. When another tribe later found her, they believed that she was a Wendigo. They killed her before she could do any more damage.

▶ Some describe Wendigo as a skeleton that has risen up from the grave. Its eyes are pushed back into their sockets, and its lips are torn and bloody.

WHERE WENDIGO PROWLS

Wendigo is a North American monster. But, if you live in a place where you have never seen snow and where citrus trees grow, you can breathe a little easier. The creature (also known as Windigo) likes colder climates—it prowls in the forests across Canada and in some Northern states, like Minnesota, North Dakota, and Montana.

▼ Locations where Wendigo has been reported.

Where—and Who—It Hunts

Wendigo skulks in the woods, carefully stalking its prey before pouncing. It hides in caves or camouflages itself and is only seen when it decides that it is ready to terrify a new victim. A person may smell the creature coming before actually seeing it. Wendigo reeks of rotten meat and decay.

Wendigo stalks its victims. It terrifies its prey until the person becomes insane and start running aimlessly through the woods. The person has no idea that he or she is heading directly toward the Wendigo. People inside dwellings are also not safe from Wendigo attacks. It can unlock cabin doors or enter **wigwams** or huts to feast on the inhabitants.

▶ *Since food can be scarce in the winter, even for Wendigo, it is intelligent enough to plan for shortages. The monster stores human flesh in caves or in treetops to feed upon later. It may also hibernate at times, resting until it is ready to feed again.*

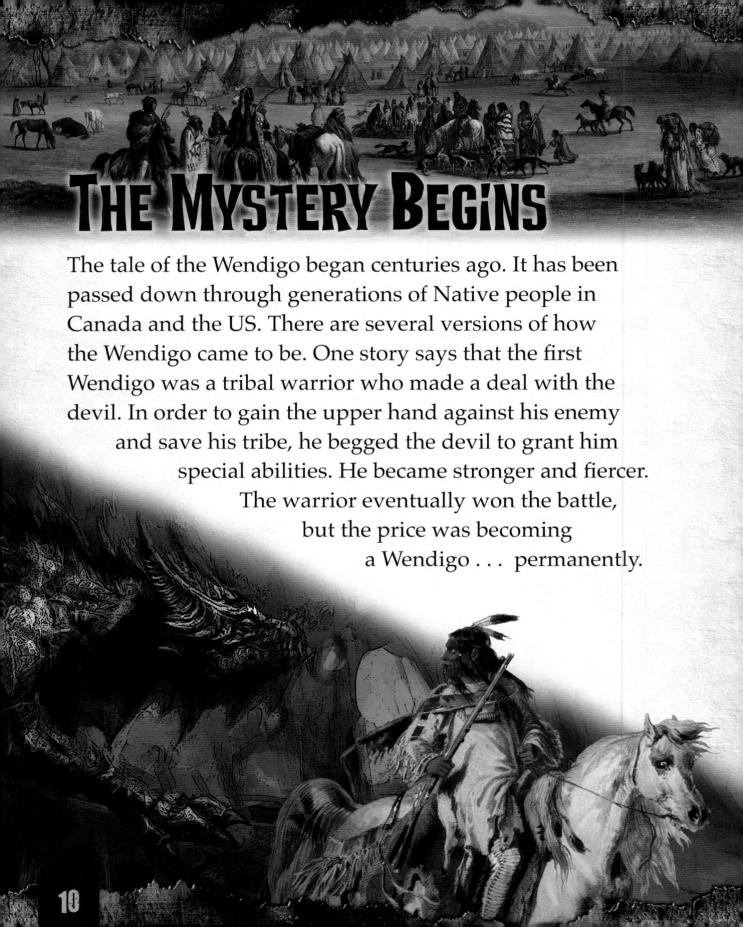

THE MYSTERY BEGINS

The tale of the Wendigo began centuries ago. It has been passed down through generations of Native people in Canada and the US. There are several versions of how the Wendigo came to be. One story says that the first Wendigo was a tribal warrior who made a deal with the devil. In order to gain the upper hand against his enemy and save his tribe, he begged the devil to grant him special abilities. He became stronger and fiercer. The warrior eventually won the battle, but the price was becoming a Wendigo . . . permanently.

Wendigo Takes Over

In another version of the origin of Wendigo, food was scarce during a particularly harsh Canadian winter. One starving tribesman went against a sacred social rule and ate the flesh of another member to survive. He became a Wendigo. According to the mythology, any human who eats the flesh of his or her own kind—a cannibal—will turn into a Wendigo or be possessed by its demon spirit.

Did You Know?

Cannibalism is a moral **taboo** in most, but not all, cultures. It is rare in the Americas, but when people are literally starving to death, it can happen as a last resort. In 1972, members of the Uruguayan rugby team were involved in a plane crash in the Andes Mountains in Chile. They were stranded for 70 days without food. The people that survived did so by eating others who had died in the crash.

▶ Cannibalism refers to humans eating the flesh or internal organs of other humans. The practice used to be common in different parts of the world. For example, Asmat people shown in this photo, and many other tribes in Papua New Guinea (near Australia) were headhunters and cannibals. Asmat people did not have contact with outsiders until the mid-twentieth century.

BECOMING A WENDIGO

In addition to cannibalism, there are several other ways that a human may become a Wendigo, according to **folklore**. Some tribes believe that spiritual possession by the creature can spread through a bite. In the rare case that a human survives an attack by a Wendigo, the spirit of the beast moves through his or her body like venom, infecting the person with the desire to eat human flesh. Eventually, the human's heart turns to ice, but not before he or she infects others.

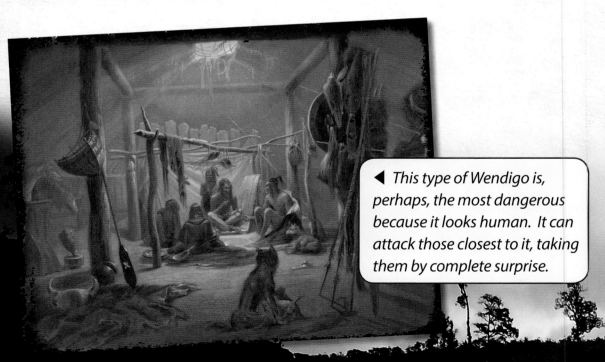

◀ This type of Wendigo is, perhaps, the most dangerous because it looks human. It can attack those closest to it, taking them by complete surprise.

SLEEP FEVER, BODY SWAPPING, AND GLUTTONY

According to lore, people can become infected by the curse of the Wendigo in their sleep. If the creature chooses them, it can enter their dreams, causing a "sleep fever." The Wendigo calls the sleeping person's name over and over again in his or her dreams, which soon become horrifying nightmares. Eventually, the creature takes over the dreamer's mind and body, contaminating the victim with a craving for humans.

Some stories tell that overly greedy humans can turn into Wendigoes. People with **gluttony** are never satisfied, just as the Wendigo is never content after it eats. Another story claims that the Wendigo spirit can take over a human body when its own wears out.

▶ Turning into a Wendigo is a terrifying experience. A person first feels the skin tightening around the bones, ripping in parts, hurting. Then the victim loses its human self and mind, becoming violent and obsessed with eating human flesh.

NATIVE LEGENDS

Wendigo is part of the Native folklore of the Algonquin people, including the Ojibwe, Cree, and Mik'Maq. Each group has a slightly different name for the beast (Wheetigo, Wendikouk, and Atchen, for example), and the stories vary, too. Some tribes believe that the creature has existed since humans have inhabited the earth and is the spirit ruler of the forest. Others consider the Wendigo to be a shape-shifter that can camouflage itself as an animal or human. Still others believe it is a giant because the more it eats, the larger it gets.

◀ *Most of the legends were not written down to be shared with outsiders. They were told as stories from generation to generation, making it difficult to get accurate accounts. Most of the published stories are "heard from someone, who heard from someone," which can lead to a lot of misinformation.*

THE SHAMAN

In some Native cultures, a Shaman is a medicine man who uses magic to cure people who are sick. The Shaman plays an important role in the story of Wendigo. It is said that the Shaman can curse a human into turning into the evil beast—or he can save someone who is in the midst of changing.

The treatment doesn't always work. To prepare the remedy, the Shaman boils fat in a large vat. He must then convince the monster to "open wide" before pouring the fat down its throat. If the Wendigo throws up its frozen heart, the transformation back to human is complete. If not . . . run.

▶ A Shaman uses dreams and visions to contact the spirit world. In some cultures, the Shaman uses magic to cure sick people and to control the future.

CAN WENDIGO BE KILLED?

Let's face it. The beast has a lot going for it in terms of survival. It's enormous and has superhuman strength and speed. Wendigo has heightened senses: it can hear a heart pounding with fear from a mile (km) away and can follow its prey by scent alone. It can also see in the dark. The creature has some other tricks up its sleeve, too. It can mimic human voices and cries for help and deafen its prey with ear-splitting screams. The creature can also heal itself from wounds almost instantly. Killing Wendigo is not easy.

▲ *Wendigo has few weaknesses, making it very difficult to kill with regular weapons. According to legend, it can only be killed by iron, steel, and silver. Some believe that fire will help protect a person from Wendigo, but only for so long.*

ALL IS NOT LOST

On the other hand, if a person walking through the woods happens to be carrying a gun loaded with silver bullets, or has a silver blade or stake, he or she may have a chance. A silver bullet or stake through the Wendigo's frozen heart is the first step. The creature then needs to be cut to pieces, burned, and the ashes scattered far apart. If this last step isn't done correctly, the Wendigo can regenerate itself, coming back as good as new.

EYEWITNESS TALE

According to one native tale, an Ojibwa Shaman named Big Goose was able to slay the Wendigo. With the help of a *Manitou* spirit, Big Goose was turned into Misshaba the giant and was able to save his people from the beast.

> ➤ To permanently destroy Wendigo, you need to follow all these steps very carefully. If the ashes are not scattered properly, the beast can come back to life.

Sightings by Europeans

Most Wendigo stories from Europeans are **second-hand accounts**, rather than sightings. In the seventeenth century, Paul Le Jeune, a French Jesuit **missionary** serving in Quebec, produced the first written account of the Wendigo. In 1636, he sent a letter back to his superiors in Rome describing the story of local Native woman who went into a spiritual trance. When she awoke, she warned that an Atchen was going to attack the village. Apparently, Le Jeune was not worried about the "beast," nor did he see it (or believe in it). He wrote the report because he was concerned that the woman's dreams were scaring his religious converts.

◀ Jesuit missionaries came to Canada in the mid-1600s. Their goal was to establish missions along the Saint Lawrence River and convert the Natives to Christianity.

THEODORE ROOSEVELT

In 1893, Theodore Roosevelt wrote a book called *The Wilderness Hunter*. In the book, he told the story of a fur trapper named Bauman. The man told Roosevelt that he was hunting with a partner, deep in the woods in Montana. Bauman and his partner walked for hours and then built a campsite to use that night. They went back to the game trail and returned later to find that their site was torn apart.

The men straightened everything out and went to sleep. In the middle of the night, they woke to a noise and a strong odor. A shadow appeared and Bauman shot at it, but missed. The next day, Bauman's partner stayed behind to take down the campsite, and Bauman went to check the last of the traps. When he returned, he found his friend at the campsite with his neck broken and four fang marks in his throat. Bauman believed that the killer was either "half-human or half-devil." When he got back to the village, residents told Bauman that the beast must have been a Wendigo.

▶ *Theodore Roosevelt became the 26th President of the United States in 1901.*

WENDIGO IN KENORA

Kenora, Ontario, Canada, has the honor of being named the "Wendigo Capital of the World," at least according to some monster enthusiasts. With many Native settlements in the area, Kenora has apparently been the site of many Wendigo incidents. You'll find no mention of the creature on the city's official website, though. Perhaps, a cannibalistic monster isn't great for tourism? Or maybe city officials believe that the Wendigo is just a myth! Still, if tourists do make it to Kenora, they often visit the Cave of Wendigo at nearby lake Mameigwess. Those who believe in the monster think that the cave attracts potential prey.

◀ *Looking for Wendigo is not the only good reason to travel to Kenora. Mameigwess is a pristine lake where tourists can enjoy great fishing for walleye and northern pike.*

WENDIGO IN POPULAR CULTURE

The city of Kenora may not want to draw attention to the legend of the Wendigo, but there are plenty of others who do. The creature first gained international attention when Algernon Blackwood published a short story, *The Wendigo*, in 1907. More recently, the beast has appeared in creepy TV shows, such as *Hannibal* and the *X-Files*, as well as less frightening shows like *Charmed*. The Wendigo was mentioned in horror-novelist Stephen King's book, *Pet Sematary*, and has appeared in Marvel comic books, fighting the Hulk. Video gamers may have noticed the Wendigo in games such as *Final Fantasy* and *Warcraft*.

EYEWITNESS TALE

In 1907, two Cree Indians, Jack Fiddler and his son, Joseph, were on trial for the murder of a woman who they had shot with silver bullets. The men admitted that they committed the murder, but said that they did it because the woman was possessed by the spirit of the Wendigo. The father–son duo believed that they had sacrificed themselves for the greater good of the tribe.

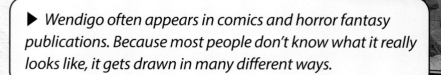

▶ *Wendigo often appears in comics and horror fantasy publications. Because most people don't know what it really looks like, it gets drawn in many different ways.*

A Wendigo Warning

Perhaps, as some people believe, the Wendigo is just a **cautionary tale** for those trying to survive in the harsh wilderness. According to tribal rules, the moral right is to choose death from starvation over cannibalism. A major goal of tribal life was to be unselfish and have self-control. People were taught that even if food was scarce, they should share. If food was plenty, they shouldn't overindulge. The story of the Wendigo may have been created as a **fable** to reinforce the rules against greed and cannibalism. The story of the Wendigo may also have been a good way for parents to keep their children from wandering too far into the woods.

Extreme Fables

The Wendigo isn't the only monster that may have been created to teach people a lesson. Other famous monster stories could have been told originally to frighten people and stop them from doing something dangerous or wrong—like fables taken to the extreme. For example, the legend of the Loch Ness Monster, which is said to inhabit a lake in Scotland, may have started thousands of years ago as a way to scare children from going too close to the lake and drowning.

▲ Before the Loch Ness Monster legend, the children of Scotland were told folktales about kelpies in the lake. These water spirits would come out of the lake looking like beautiful horses, and tempt humans to ride them. Once a person mounted the horse, the kelpie would take its victim into the water to drown.

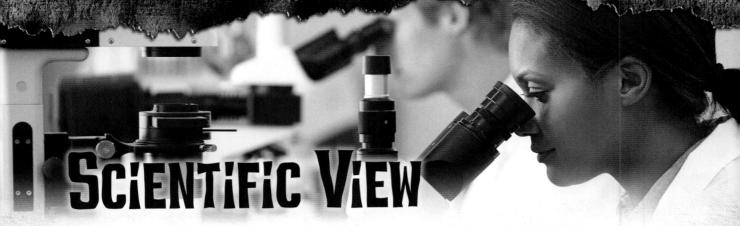

Scientific View

Most scientists do not believe that Wendigoes exist. There has never been any solid evidence for researchers to study: no body, no hair, and no **DNA**. There is no proof of its existence, except for a handful of (mostly secondhand) eyewitness tales and legends that may have originated merely as warnings in the form of stories. Finding proof of the Wendigo is probably not high on most scientists' "To Do" lists.

◀ The Wendigo would be a prime catch for cryptozoologists. These researchers look for evidence of animals that have not yet been proven to exist (cryptids). Cryptozoologists look at photos, take casts of footprints, and send DNA samples to labs. Sometimes they even head to locations where a sighting has been reported to search for legendary beasts using technology like motion-sensitive cameras and night-vision goggles. Compared to monsters like Bigfoot, there hasn't been much to find in the case of the Wendigo.

Wendigo Psychosis

Scientists are also skeptical about whether or not a "disorder" that's been associated with the beast is real. In the early 1900s, psychologists began diagnosing some Native people with an illness called Wendigo Psychosis. Individuals with signs of the psychiatric condition feared that they were turning into Wendigoes and craved human flesh. Symptoms usually began after periods of starvation during the winter months. Sufferers often went to the tribe's Shaman for help. In some cases, these individuals were executed. Scientists are not sure whether the disorder exists or is caused by a misunderstanding about Native legend.

▶ Winters in the early 1900s were often harsh and food was scarce. When it ran out, Native communities faced long months of starvation. It was not always easy to keep alert.

WENDIGO COUSINS

Could the Wendigo be a relative of Bigfoot? Over the years, thousands of people have claimed to see a giant, hairy apeman-type creature in the woods across North America. They call it Bigfoot or Sasquatch. Other than the fact that both Bigfoot and Wendigo are tall and live in the forest, they have little in common. At 500 pounds (227 kg), Bigfoot is obese compared to the skin-and-bones Wendigo. And the creature is not nearly as ruthless. If Bigfoot tales are true, its biggest crime is kidnapping. Apparently Bigfoot once captured a man and then took care of him in a cave, later returning him home safe and unharmed.

◀ *Some communities believe that Bigfoot is part of another Native tribe. Others consider it to be a shy animal that is scared of humans. Some tribes worship the creature, believing that it has supernatural abilities and is a guardian of the forest. Yet other tribes consider Bigfoot a monster that attacks humans and steals children.*

WEREWOLVES

Wendigo may be more similar to Werewolves (also known as Lycanthropes) than Bigfoot. Werewolves are legendary humans that are able to shape-shift into a wolf or **hybrid** of a wolf and human. Werewolf folklore began in Europe and later spread to the new world. In more recent stories, the werewolf changes form under the power of the full moon and can be killed by a silver bullet. In some cultures, becoming a werewolf is the result of a curse brought on by engaging in cannibalism. Sound familiar? Similar to Wendigo Psychosis, the psychiatric condition called clinical lycanthropy is when a person believes him or herself to be a werewolf.

▲ *Werewolves are active at night. They are said to change back to human form in daylight.*

WHAT DO YOU THINK?

Now that you have read all about the Wendigo, what do you think? Is the monster out there roaming the North American woods in search of its next meal, or does it live only in the minds of storytellers? Native Canadians and Americans aren't the only groups with legends about cannibalism. In Greek mythology, Chronos eats his children, for example. The Huli people of Papua New Guinea, also tell stories about an ancient race of giants (Baya Horo) who ate human flesh. Cannibalism makes for interesting stories.

◄ *Some legends say that the Wendigo's favorite part of its human victim is the brain.*

FIND OUT FOR YOURSELF

If you want to go on a search for the truth, start in the most obvious places—those named after the beast. There is a town called Windigo in Quebec, Canada, and as mentioned earlier, you'll find the Cave of Wendigo near Kenora, Ontario.

In Ontario's Algonquin Provincial Park, you can set up camp on Wendigo Lake. First, you'll have to drive deep into the woods down a long gravel road. Then, leave your car behind, canoe in further, and trek deeper into the woods. It is stunningly silent on the lake at night, except for the occasional sound of birds. On moonless nights, the woods are a black sheet. The question is, with all that you now know about the beast, would you feel safe camping on a lake named Wendigo?

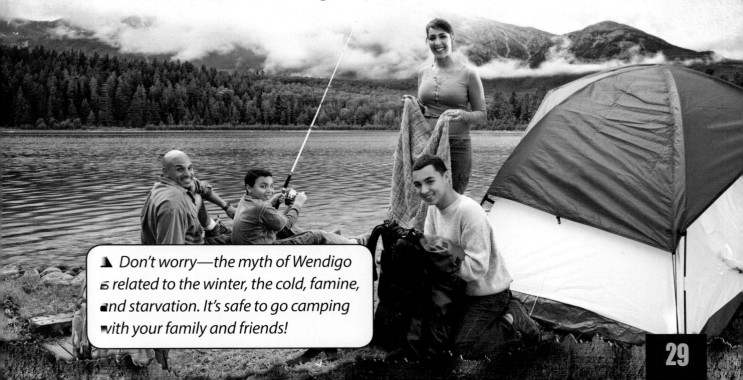

▲ *Don't worry—the myth of Wendigo is related to the winter, the cold, famine, and starvation. It's safe to go camping with your family and friends!*

GLOSSARY

cannibal (KA-nih-bul) One that eats the flesh of its own kind.

carnivores (KAHR-neh-vorz) Animals that eat meat.

cautionary tale (KAW-shuh-neh-ree TAYL) A story that gives a warning to the listener.

continuum (kun-TIN-yoo-um) Range or series of things that are slightly different from each other and that exist between two different possibilities.

DNA (DEE IN AY) A substance that carries genetic information in the cells of plants and animals.

fable (FAY-bull) A short story that usually is about animals and that is intended to teach a lesson.

folklore (FOHK-lor) Traditional customs, beliefs, stories, and sayings; ideas or stories that are not true but that many people have heard or read.

gluttony (GLUH-tuh-nee) Excess in eating or drinking.

hybrid (HY-brud) An animal or plant that is produced from two animals or plants of different kinds.

hypertrichosis (hy-pur-tri-KOH-sus) A hereditary condition causes rapid hair growth all over the body, including on the hands and face.

manitou (MA-nuh-too) (Algonquin) A supernatural force.

missionary (MIH-shuh-ner-ee) A person who is sent to a foreign country to do religious work.

second-hand accounts (SEH-kund-HAND uh-KOWNTZ) Stories that were heard from someone else; the teller did not see/ experience it for himself or herself.

taboo (ta-BOO) Banned on grounds of morality or taste.

wigwams (WIG-wahmz) Huts of the American Indians of the Great Lakes region and eastward having typically an arched framework of poles overlaid with bark, mats, or hides.

FOR MORE INFORMATION

FURTHER READING

Ferrell, David L. *Shape-Shifters!* Jr. Graphic Monster Stories. New York: PowerKids Press, 2014.

McCall, Gerrie. *Ancient Legends.* Monsters & Myths. New York: Gareth Stevens, 2011.

Peterson, Megan Cooley. *Haunting Urban Legends.* Scared! Mankato, MN: Capstone Press, 2014.

WEBSITES

Due to the changing nature of Internet links, PowerKids Press has developed an online list of websites related to the subject of this book. This site is updated regularly. Please use this link to access the list:

www.powerkidslinks.com/mymo/wend/

INDEX